BIG RED TUB

To Theo William and Maya Josephine—J.J.
For Rebecca Anne—A.R.

Text copyright © 2004 by Julia Jarman
Illustrations copyright © 2004 by Adrian Reynolds
First published in Great Britain in 2004 by Orchard Books London.

Library of Congress Cataloging-in-Publication Data available
ISBN 0-439-67232-5

10 9 8 7 6 5 4 3 2 1   04 05 06 07 08
First Scholastic edition, December 2004
Reinforced Binding for Library Use
Printed in Singapore

BIG RED TUB

BY JULIA JARMAN

ILLUSTRATED BY ADRIAN REYNOLDS

Orchard Books
New York
An Imprint of Scholastic Inc.

Stan and Stella in the big red tub.
I splash!
You splash!

Splash! Splash! Splash!
Bubbles in the bath,
water on the floor.

But who's this
scratching at the door?

"Hi there, kids! Can I come for a swim?"
"'Course you can, Dog. Just dive in!"

Dog dives in, front feet first.

Suds rise high, bubbles burst!

Dog, Stan, and Stella in the big red tub—
    I splash!
    You splash!

"Hi there, kids! Can I have a wash?"
"Leap in, Lion. Slish and slosh!"

Lion leaps in and starts to scrub.

Suds rise high—rub-a-dub-dub!

Lion, Dog, Stan, and Stella in the tub—
I splash!
You splash!

"Hello, kids! Can I come for a paddle?"
"'Course you can, Duck! Dibble and dabble!"

Duck dibble-dabbles at a quacking pace.

Bubbles fly all over the place!

Duck, Lion, Dog, Stan, and Stella in the bath—
I splash!
You splash!

Turtle hurtles in.
"Can I have a dip?"

Pursued by Penguin.
"I want to flip!"

Giraffe races in.
"Make room for me,
I'm being followed!"

Who can it be?

It's Hippopotamus!

He slips on the floor!

He slides under the tub!

Which goes

Sloosh

through the door and . . .

. . . down the stairs—so very fast!

Kangaroo wants a ride,

but the tub shoots past!

But Kanga's determined.
She takes a bound,
so the big red tub suddenly...

It flies twice 'round the world,
over mountain and plain.

Till a flock of flamingos . . .

. . . tows it home again!

Bubbles in the tub,
water on the floor.
Who is THIS coming in the door?

It's Mom!
Rubba-dubba-giggle,
rubba-dubba-dub.

"Let's tell Mom about
our big red tub!"

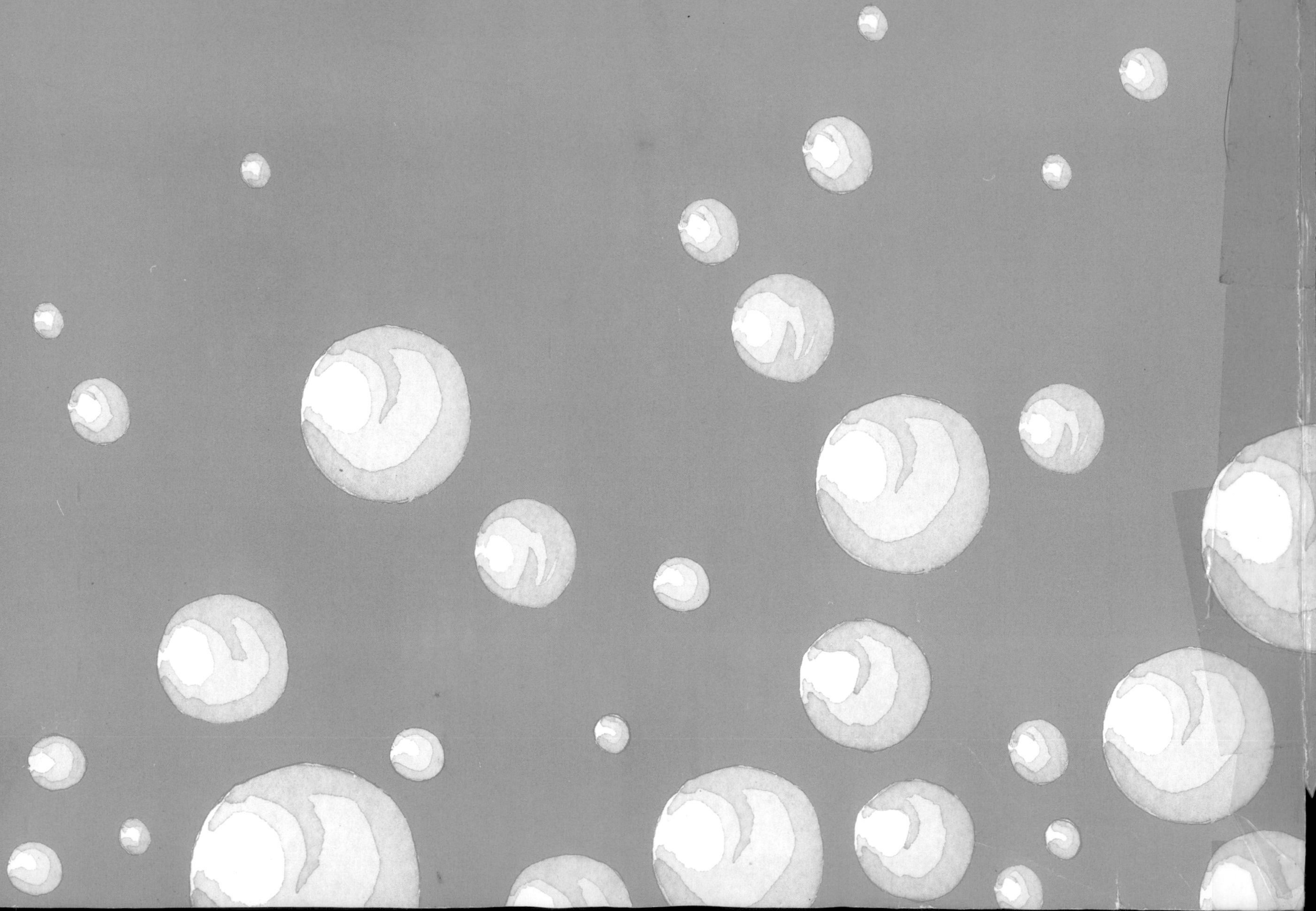